Benny Bear

by Miriam Sklar

ISBN: 978-1-338-75069-0
Illustrated by John Lund

Published by Scholastic Inc., 557 Broadway, New York, NY 10012

10 9 8 7 6 5 4 68 25 26 27/0

Printed in Jiaxing, China. First printing, January 2021.

Benny Bear has a hoop.

Benny Bear has a scoop.

Benny Bear has a sock.

Benny Bear has a block.

Benny Bear has a snack.

Benny Bear has a cap.

Benny Bear has a bear!